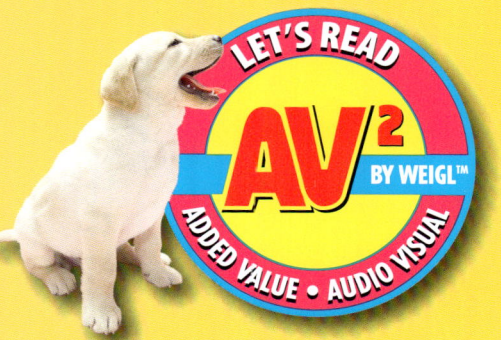

AV² provides enriched content that supplements and complements this book. Weigl's AV² books strive to create inspired learning and engage young minds in a total learning experience.

Your AV² Media Enhanced books come alive with...

 **Audio** Listen to sections of the book read aloud.

 **Video** Watch informative video clips.

 **Embedded Weblinks** Gain additional information for research.

 **Try This!** Complete activities and hands-on experiments.

 **Key Words** Study vocabulary, and complete a matching word activity.

 **Quizzes** Test your knowledge.

 **Slide Show** View images and captions, and prepare a presentation.

... and much, much more!

Go to www.av2books.com, and enter this book's unique code.

BOOK CODE

G723239

AV² by Weigl brings you media enhanced books that support active learning.

Published by AV² by Weigl
350 5th Avenue, 59th Floor New York, NY 10118
Website: www.av2books.com

Copyright ©2017 AV² by Weigl
All rights reserved. No part of this publication may be reproduced, stored in a retrieval system, or transmitted in any form or by any means, electronic, mechanical, photocopying, recording, or otherwise, without the prior written permission of Weigl Publishers Inc.

Library of Congress Control Number: 2015958824

ISBN 978-1-4896-4749-8 (hardcover)
ISBN 978-1-4896-4811-2 (softcover)
ISBN 978-1-4896-4750-4 (multi-user eBook)

Printed in the United States of America in Brainerd, Minnesota
1 2 3 4 5 6 7 8 9 0 19 18 17 16 15

122015
041215

Project Coordinator: Heather Kissock
Designer: Terry Paulhus

Every reasonable effort has been made to trace ownership and to obtain permission to reprint copyright material. The publisher would be pleased to have any errors or omissions brought to its attention so that they may be corrected in subsequent printings.

The publisher acknowledges Corbis Images, Alamy, Minden Pictures, and Getty Images as the primary image suppliers for this title.

Squirrels

In this book, I will tell you about their

home **food** **family** and **how they grow up.**

3

One day last summer, I was playing in my treehouse when I saw a hole in the tree.

I looked inside and saw a whole bunch of leaves and moss. When I told my dad about it, he said that it was a squirrel's den.

5

My dad told me that a woodpecker used to live in the hole. He said squirrels often make their homes in old woodpecker holes.

My dad said I could watch the squirrel from my treehouse, but that I should not get too close to it.

I climbed into my treehouse every day to see what the squirrel was doing. Once I saw it chase another squirrel away.

My dad said that the squirrel may be going to have babies. He said I should be careful around the squirrel or it might chase me.

My dad told me that we might have to wait until early fall to see the babies. I did not mind, but I sure wanted to see those babies.

One night, I heard a chirping sound. I got my dad to shine a flashlight into the hole. We saw four babies. Their eyes were closed, and they had no fur.

12

It took about three weeks for the babies to grow in their fur. It was another two weeks before they opened their eyes.

Even though they could see, they stayed in the den with their mother.

There was a big storm yesterday, and the wind bent a lot of branches. I was worried about the babies.

I saw the mother carrying her babies out of the den one at a time. She put them in another hole lower on the tree.

The babies stayed in their new home and did not go back to the other den. I did not mind. I could see this den much better.

One day, I saw the babies running in and out of the den. Their mother watched them as they played.

The young squirrels were starting to get bigger. They were becoming very fast climbers. They could even switch trees by running along the branches.

One day, I saw one of the squirrels switch trees carrying a pinecone in its mouth. My dad said it was starting to store food for winter.

It started to get really cold. The young squirrels stopped coming back to the den.

My dad said that they were old enough to live on their own. They had likely made dens of their own in other trees.

The next summer, my dad called me into the backyard.

There was another family of squirrels living in the tree.

KEY WORDS

Research has shown that as much as 65 percent of all written material published in English is made up of 300 words. These 300 words cannot be taught using pictures or learned by sounding them out. They must be recognized by sight. This book contains 102 common sight words to help young readers improve their reading fluency and comprehension. This book also teaches young readers several important content words, such as proper nouns. These words are paired with pictures to aid in learning and improve understanding.

Page	Sight Words First Appearance
4	a, about, and, day, he, I, in, it, last, leaves, my, of, one, said, saw, that, the, tree, was, when
7	but, close, could, from, get, homes, live, make, me, not, often, old, should, their, to, too, used, watch
9	another, around, away, be, every, have, into, may, might, once, or, see, what
10	did, eyes, four, got, had, no, sound, they, those, until, we, were
13	before, even, for, grow, mother, three, took, two, with
15	at, big, her, on, out, put, she, them, there, time
16	as, back, go, much, new, other, this
19	along, by, food, its, very, young
20	enough, made, own, really, started
22	next
23	family

Page	Content Words First Appearance
4	bunch, dad, den, hole, moss, squirrel, summer, treehouse
7	woodpecker
9	babies
10	fall, flashlight, fur
13	weeks
15	branches, wind, storm
19	climbers, mouth, pinecone, winter
22	backyard

Check out www.av2books.com for activities, videos, audio clips, and more!

 Go to www.av2books.com.

 Enter book code. G723239

 Fuel your imagination online!

www.av2books.com

What do I see?

Bobbie Kalman

 Crabtree Publishing Company
www.crabtreebooks.com

Created by Bobbie Kalman

Author and Editor-in-Chief
Bobbie Kalman

Educational consultants
Elaine Hurst
Reagan Miller
Joan King

Editors
Joan King
Reagan Miller
Kathy Middleton

Proofreader
Crystal Sikkens

Design
Bobbie Kalman
Katherine Berti

Photo research
Bobbie Kalman

Production coordinator
Katherine Berti

Prepress technician
Katherine Berti

Photographs
BigStockPhoto: p. 7
Other photographs by Shutterstock

Library and Archives Canada Cataloguing in Publication

Kalman, Bobbie, 1947-
　　　　What do I see? / Bobbie Kalman.

(My world)
ISBN 978-0-7787-9419-6 (bound).--ISBN 978-0-7787-9463-9 (pbk.)

　　　　1. Vision--Juvenile literature. I. Title. II. Series: My world
(St. Catharines, Ont.)

QP475.7.K34 2010　　　　j612.8'4　　　　C2009-906055-8

Library of Congress Cataloging-in-Publication Data

Kalman, Bobbie.
　What do I see? / Bobbie Kalman.
　　p. cm. -- (My world)
　ISBN 978-0-7787-9463-9 (pbk. : alk. paper) -- ISBN 978-0-7787-9419-6
(reinforced library binding : alk. paper)
　1. Habitat (Ecology)--Juvenile literature. I. Title. II. Series.

QH541.14.K3498 2010
590--dc22

2009040957

Crabtree Publishing Company

www.crabtreebooks.com　　　　1-800-387-7650

Printed in China/122009/CT20091009

Copyright © **2010 CRABTREE PUBLISHING COMPANY.** All rights reserved. No part of this publication may be reproduced, stored in a retrieval system or be transmitted in any form or by any means, electronic, mechanical, photocopying, recording, or otherwise, without the prior written permission of Crabtree Publishing Company. In Canada: We acknowledge the financial support of the Government of Canada through the Book Publishing Industry Development Program (BPIDP) for our publishing activities.

Published in Canada
Crabtree Publishing
616 Welland Ave.
St. Catharines, Ontario
L2M 5V6

Published in the United States
Crabtree Publishing
PMB 59051
350 Fifth Avenue, 59th Floor
New York, New York 10118

Published in the United Kingdom
Crabtree Publishing
Maritime House
Basin Road North, Hove
BN41 1WR

Published in Australia
Crabtree Publishing
386 Mt. Alexander Rd.
Ascot Vale (Melbourne)
VIC 3032

Words to know

bee

bunny

butterfly

chimpanzee

dolphin

raccoon

seashell

What do you see?
What do I see?

I see a bunny looking at me.

What do you see?
What do I see?

I see two raccoons living in a tree.

What do you see?
What do I see?

I see a baby chimpanzee.
He is not looking at me.

What do you see?
What do I see?

I see dolphins jumping in the sea.

What do you see?
What do I see?

I see two butterflies and a bee.

Do you see a young girl sleeping inside a seashell?

Is she really in there?
I will never tell!

Notes for adults

Seeing the "seer"
What do I see? helps children identify things that they see, as well as use their imaginations. Ask what the children see in this book. How many answered that they saw a child pointing or looking at an animal?

What have they seen?
How many of the animals in the book have the children themselves seen? Ask them to tell stories about the bunnies, raccoons, dolphins, or chimpanzees that they have seen. Which picture in the book is not real? Ask them to describe what they think the word "real" means. What things have they seen that are real and not real?

"I spy with my little eye"
A favorite children's game is "I spy, with my little eye, something that is…" This simple game can be used to teach colors, math skills (using shapes), the alphabet (things that start with certain letters), and sizes.

How do you see?
Ask children how many different ways they see. Some answers might be: with their eyes, with glasses, through binoculars, and so on. Invite them to look at common objects through a magnifying glass. Ask them to explain what they see and how it is different from what they see when they look at the same object with just their eyes. Suggested objects: a leaf, a stuffed toy, a page in a book, or their skin.